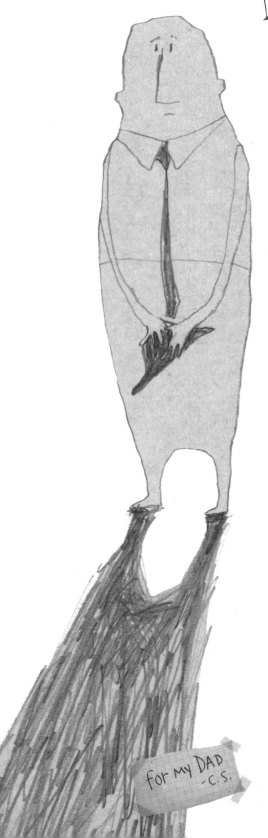

MY DAD IS BIG AND STRONG, BUT...

A BEDTIME STORY

By Coralie Saudo

Illustrated by
Kris Di Giacomo

for my DAD -C.S.

ENCHANTED LION BOOKS
NEW YORK

My dad
is big and strong, but every
night it's the

same old story.

And this is how it begins:

At first, I try
to be nice:

"Dad," I say, "it's already quite late. You need to go to sleep now in order to be in good shape for tomorrow."

But often it's right at that moment that things

get complicated...

"NO NO NO,

yells Dad as he runs
around the house.

So I try a little
firmness.

"All right, Dad,

but I'm not going
to run after you.

It's not time
for games.

Come sit here with me and
I'll read you a story."

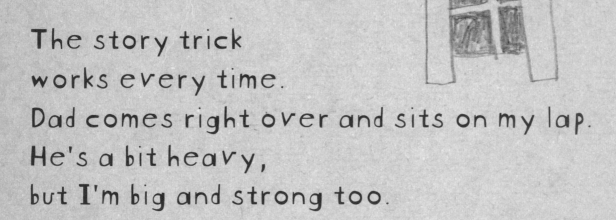

The story trick
works every time.
Dad comes right over and sits on my lap.
He's a bit heavy,
but I'm big and strong too.

The problem comes when I finish
the story and say:

"Off to bed
with you!"

Then Daddy holds me
tight and begs with all
his might for:

"One More Story
pleeease,
just one more!"

And when he looks at me
with those pleading puppy dog eyes,
I give in every time
and read him another story.

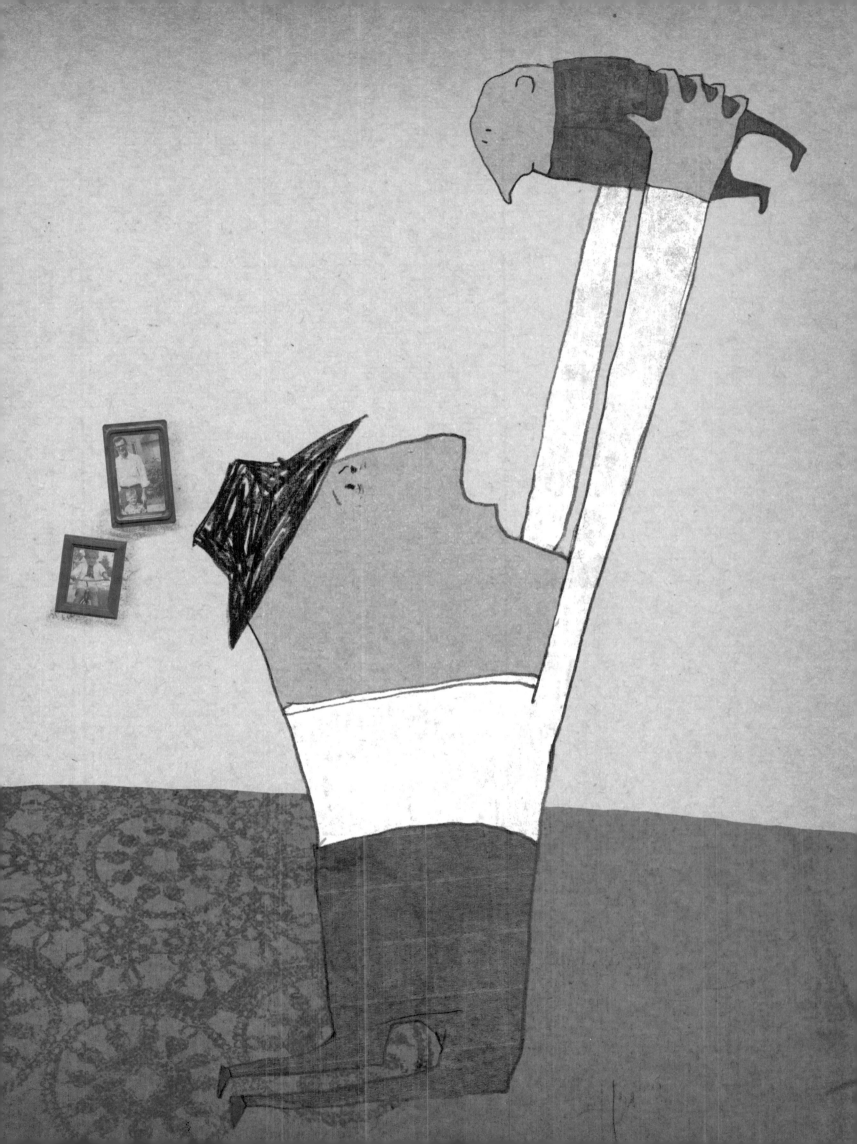

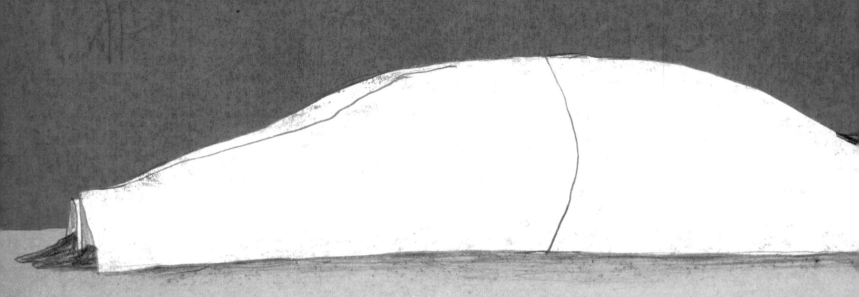

When that one is done,
Daddy always asks me for just one more...

But enough is enough!

"Dad," I say.
"We said one story, and we've already
read two. That's enough for tonight.
Now off to bed! I am going to tuck you in."

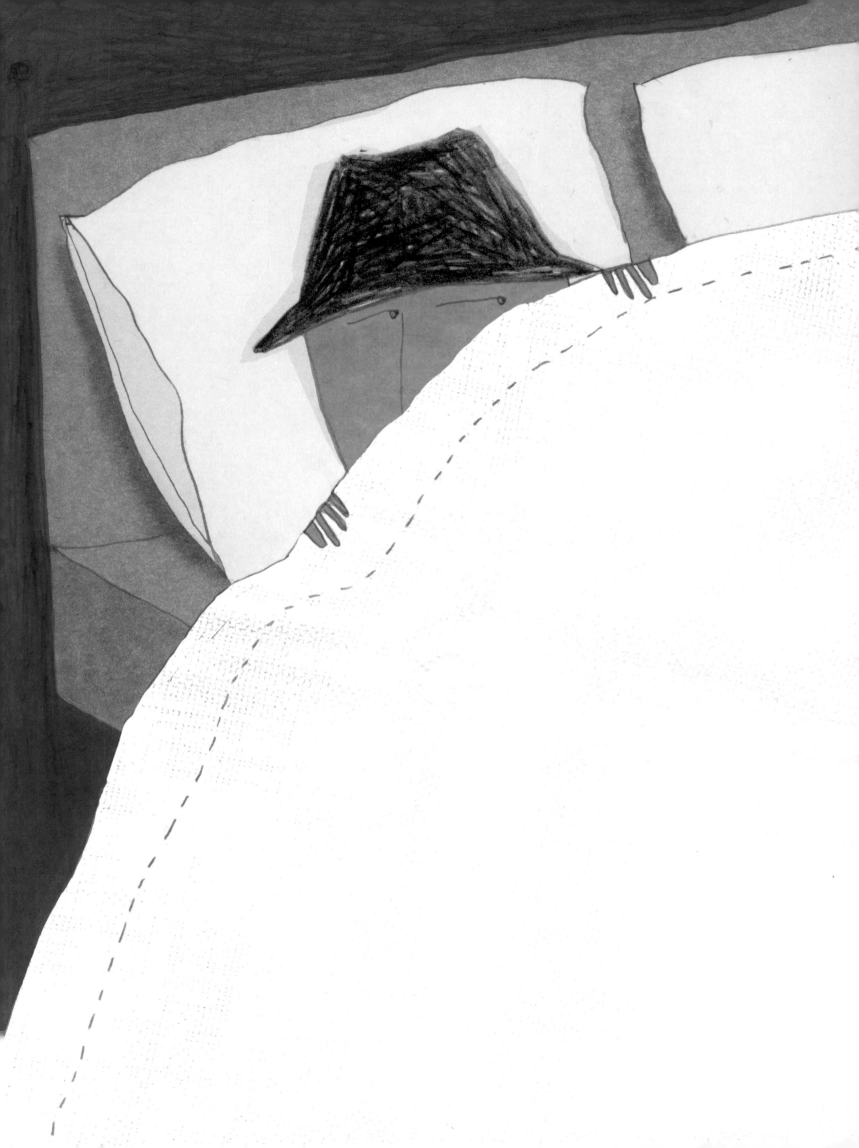

As Daddy slides under the covers,
he looks as though he's about
to cry, and then I tell myself:

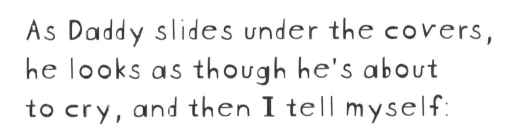
" Hang on,
We're almost there"

Because a Dad who doesn't
want to go to sleep is exhausting!

I would love to climb into my own bed
and go to sleep, but if I head to my bedroom now,
Daddy will come after me and sweetly ask:

"Son?
Can I sleep in here
with you?"

And then putting him to bed again
will be mission impossible!

So, he needs to fall asleep in his own room.

"Good night, dear Dad,
give me a big kiss.
Sweet dreams, sleep tight."

"Good

night,"

says Dad in a
small, faraway voice.

But as soon as I stand on tiptoes to turn off the light, I hear:

My dad is
big

and

strong,

but he's afraid of the dark.

And so **I** leave on the lamp
outside his room until he falls asleep.

the
end.